The Feeling of Water

The Feeling of Water

A Novella

Book Two in the Alice Brickstone Series

Tyler Pike

Copyright © 2016 Tyler Pike

All rights reserved.

ISBN-10: 0-9945794-1-1
ISBN-13: 978-0-9945794-1-6
Ebook ISBN-10: 0-9945794-0-3
Ebook ISBN-13: 978-0-9945794-0-9

www.tylerpikebooks.com

This book is a work of fiction. All characters are drawn from the author's imagination and are not to be construed as real. Any resemblance to actual persons, living or dead, is coincidental.

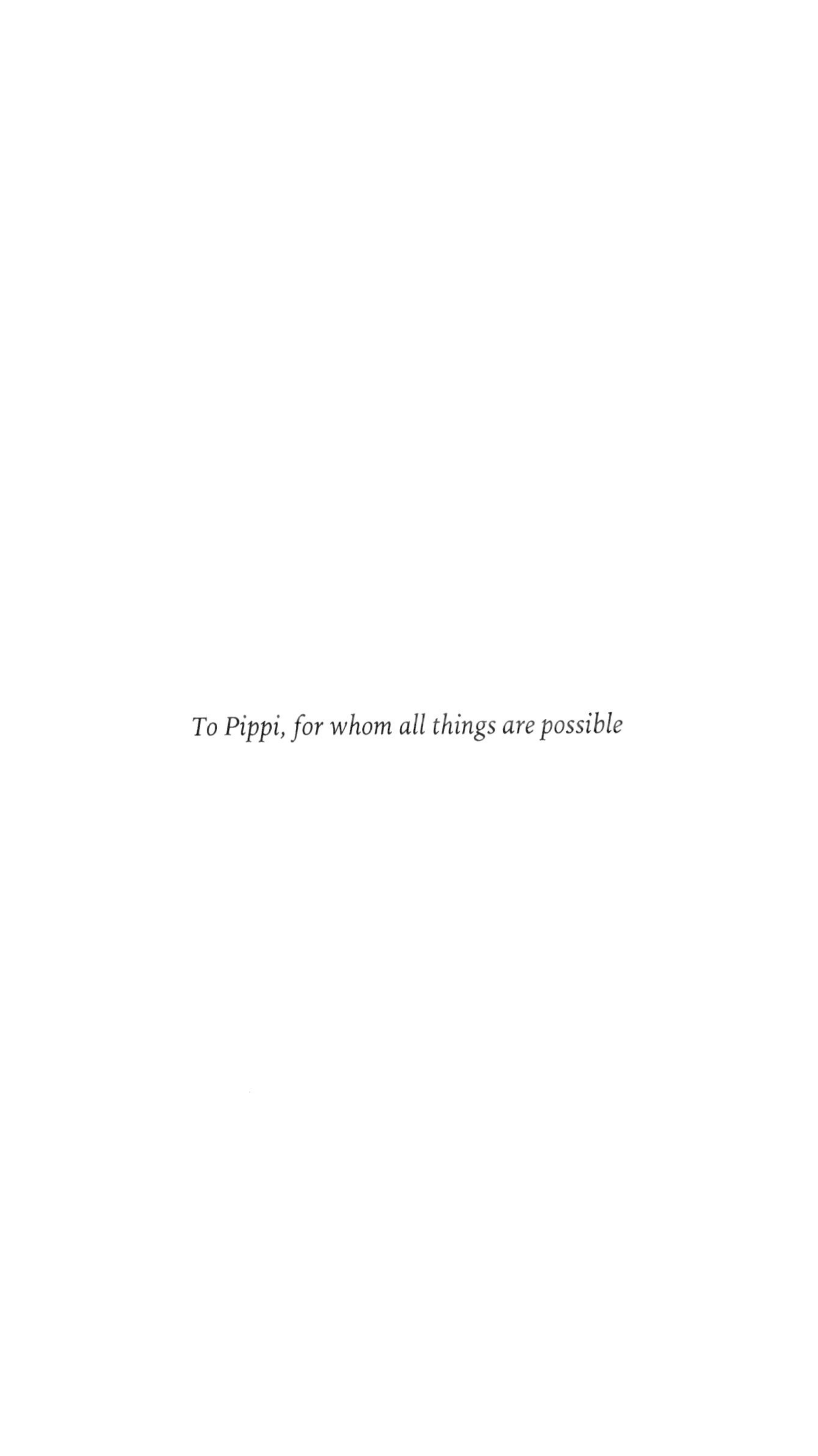
To Pippi, for whom all things are possible

CONTENTS

ABOUT THE BOOK

The Feeling of Water is a novella in the Alice Brickstone thriller series. Although the events in this book take place just after those recounted in *Girl in the Air*, these first two Alice Brickstone books can be read in any order. Neither one contains any spoilers for the other.

ACKNOWLEDGMENTS

A heartfelt vote of thanks to my editor, the irreplaceable Tom Flood.

My wife Tamsin lives the writing of all my books. Without your ideas and your encouragement, this book would have never come into being. As usual, it feels woefully insufficient to thank you here, but a failure to mention you here would be worse. So, thank you!

CHAPTER 1

The temperature dropped dramatically in five minutes, as Karan knew it would. In the winter it had been cold all the time and she welcomed the warmer days of spring with the enthusiasm of a hypothermic crash victim, which she in fact had been six months ago.

She loved the dry heat of the Colorado midday sun on her skin but the warmth of the spring always plunged itself back into winter in the span of five minutes, same time every day. She felt even colder because of the constant icy bluster of the river that ran alongside the restaurant where she ate every evening with her dad.

All the other people on the riverside deck were covering bare shoulders and donning jackets as they continued to smile at their dates and families and clink beer glasses but the huge, muscular woman on the far side of the deck was well into her second or third milkshake and appeared oblivious to the cold. The woman leaned on the wooden rail, shunning company, staring at the rapids below. Or maybe she wasn't even looking at anything at all.

She turned and caught Karan staring.

Karan realized she had misjudged the woman's age, who was probably thirty or less: maybe twenty. She noticed an angry scar on the milkshake girl's forehead.

Karan looked away, embarrassed.

"Beautiful evening." Karan was startled by a sonorous voice from behind her. She turned, expecting to face a huge mountain of a man, but she was even more surprised when confronted with a skinny, short guy wearing a white t-shirt, holding a beer and smiling at her.

"I guess," Karan replied, though she felt it was just cold.

Karan knew she should be flattered to be spoken to by any man, especially given her condition—she could hardly look at herself in the mirror—but this guy was not her type.

"It gets dark in this valley so early," he said. "Up here, we get sunset during happy hour, while all the poor suckers in Denver have to wait."

"I guess," she said, though guessing was all she could do. She had no memory of any bars in Denver, no memory of anything before the accident six months ago.

"The river is running clear and low. It's been a dry spring." He stood up on his tip-toes and leaned over the railing to see better.

"Whoah." His voice grew even deeper. "Will you look at that. Hey, come here," he said, gesturing to Karan. "Check it out."

Karan reluctantly stood up from her chair, resolved to give a cursory look at whatever he wanted to show her, and then use the opportunity to make her exit.

"That's a rainbow trout hovering behind those rocks right there." He pointed when Karan leaned over to look. "He just jumped for a mayfly. They often hatch in the late afternoons."

As she stared at the icy-white water, Karan's vision fractured and she was no longer standing safely on a deck during happy hour, but was immersed, surrounded by icy, violently disturbed water. She was fighting to breathe, struggling against certain and quickly-approaching death, her body bleeding out into the same water she was drowning in. Her chest was pierced with something and her face had been so badly smashed, she wasn't even confident there was a face left hanging on her at all.

Two heavy hands were forcing her head down deeper into the turbulence. She managed to catch a glimpse of her murderer through the disturbed river mud and bubbles—a man in a backwards baseball cap, clinging to his head despite the force of the current. It was her father.

She decided she must ask him why, before she died. She decided she would use the last ounce of her life's energy to take him around the throat, draw him toward her ruined face, and scream at him, underwater, the single word: "Why?"

As soon as her fingers touched him, she knew he was dead, and had already been dead. It had only been the current forcing his hands on her. They would soon be dead together.

As soon as he drifted away, he returned, or was it a different man? It must be her father.

He had the same cap, worn backwards. Perhaps the other man hadn't been her father after all. This one was the real one. This one was pulling her out of the river.

"Easy. Easy. Are you okay?" a deep voice was asking her. The skinny man was standing above her, and they were back on the bar's deck overlooking the river, droning its freezing hush noise as it pushed against rocks and rolled down toward the plains. Above him was the milkshake girl, looking down at Karan with a face full of disdain. Karan rolled her head left and right, and confirmed there were no dead people around anywhere. As soon as the last vestiges of Karan's hallucination had passed, and she had pushed herself up again, milkshake girl rolled her eyes and walked away. She must have thought Karan was drunk.

"Let me help you into a sitting position," the skinny guy said. "You just up and fell over. You passed out. What's your name?"

"Karan," she said without thinking. "That's Karan with 'an' instead of 'en.'" Wait, she thought to herself. What was she doing? She must have gotten too used to answering doctors robotically when they asked her name. She immediately regretted divulging her name to this creepy guy.

As Karan scrambled to stand, he pushed her down. "No, no, no. You gotta stay low. I'll call an ambulance."

As soon as he forced her back down, the milkshake girl dashed over quicker than a squirrel and swept him away with the back of her left arm, knocking him toward the glass doors of the bar.

"Here," she said, holding out a hand.

Karan took her hand and stood up. Looking into her eyes was like looking into a miniaturized astronomical event. They were blue-green, like the river, but the irises spindled outward in a starburst pattern until they were met by a deep blue circle bordering the clear whites of her eyes.

"You don't remember anything, do you?"

As she lifted her chin to respond, Karan realized how tall milkshake girl really was. At five-ten, Karan was tall, but Karan's eyes were on the same level as this girl's mouth.

"What do you mean?" Karan asked.

"Never mind. You okay? I gotta go."

"No. I'm not okay, but thanks for chasing that guy off." Karan looked around and saw he had shuffled off, scowling, to the bar.

"I don't think he's coming back,"

milkshake girl observed. "You black out often?"

"No."

"Okay."

"Actually, I didn't just black out. I think I was hallucinating."

"Sucks," milkshake girl said, her eyes wandering again. She seemed to be getting bored.

"I think the water brought it on. That guy said something about the water. I've always been terrified of water."

"Oh. That's weird. I thought you couldn't remember anything. Hey, how old are you?"

"That's an odd question to ask someone who you just peeled off the deck."

"Sorry. Okay, see ya," she said and started walking away.

Karan realized she didn't want the girl to go away.

"I'm twenty-one," she told the back of milkshake girl's head.

Milkshake girl turned and said, reluctantly, "I'm Alice."

Alice hesitated, but walked back. "Hey, listen, I'm sixteen, and I need a twenty-one-year-old person to sit in my car while I drive. I gotta get fifty hours of supervised driving logged in before they give me my full driver's license."

Now it was Karan's turn to look skeptical.

"You have got to be kidding me. You look at least twenty."

When Alice didn't seem to understand, Karan added, "I bet you get that all the time."

Clearly, Alice didn't think so. "Whatever," Alice said after an awkward pause. "Anyway, I think I can help you with the water thing. I'm kind of a good swimmer. You sit with me in my car for a few hours, or at least say you did, and I'll teach you how to swim."

Karan considered the odd request, and then looked inside the restaurant where her father, with his backwards baseball cap, was looking at her wide-eyed. He didn't like her to socialize. He said it was bad for her recovery to get too worked up. Apparently he had been too busy with his beer to notice her passing out on the deck.

He rushed out, as she expected, and put himself between Karan and her new "friend."

"You okay, honey?" He was squinting, wary.

"Yeah, Dad, I'm fine. This is Alice."

"Pleased to meet you," he said, though he clearly didn't mean it.

Alice didn't respond.

"We should be heading home." Dad was already guiding Karan toward the doors. It had been months since she actually needed help walking. She felt fine now, physically, but old habits die hard and she didn't mind her dad doting over her now and then. But now was not then.

"Hey, Dad," Karan said with a firmness she didn't feel, "I'll catch up with you at the car. I just want to say goodbye to Alice."

He looked at Alice skeptically, smiled with only half of his face, and walked off through the doors to pay.

"I'm sorry about that," Karan said to Alice. "He's overly protective."

"That's your father? The one you thought was drowning you but who ended up drowned?"

Karan paused, confused.

"What the hell?" she finally exclaimed. "How do you know? I didn't tell you all that."

"Or was he the one pulling you out of the water?"

Karan looked at Alice's mesmerizing eyes and decided she wasn't playing some game. Perhaps Karan had mumbled that stuff when she was unconscious.

"It was just a hallucination," Karan said.

"Okay. So do you want my help getting over that water thing or not?"

Karan looked at her dad, who had finished paying for their dinner and was looking back through the window at her expectantly.

"Alright. Where is your pool?"

"Don't worry about it. I'll pick you up at five tomorrow morning. Where do you live?"

"Five. AM. Tell me you don't swim at five AM."

"I don't swim at five AM. I'm used to being in the water by six. I'm only here for a few weeks and I'm trying to maintain the same training schedule as my regular swim team back in Hardrock where I live. I do an evening session too. I'm going to the pool now too, if you'd rather come now."

"No, I gotta get home. Okay, pick me up in the parking lot here."

"Cool. See you tomorrow at five."

Karan frowned as she watched Alice stride purposefully away. Karan didn't fully trust her, but she seemed to be someone who knew where she was going. Maybe some of it would rub off on Karan.

As she walked toward her father, Karan realized Alice didn't even know her name.

CHAPTER 2

Karan couldn't remember anything about her past but she was pretty sure she had never done anything this stupid before. Getting up at four AM was excruciating enough, but then she had to sneak out of the house without waking her dad, walk thirty minutes down a mountain road through the charcoal darkness, tempting the mountain lions to eat her, and then sit down in this empty, black parking lot waiting for a complete stranger to pick her up and take her God-knows-where to learn how to overcome the deepest fear she had.

Karan kicked a rock in the dirt and considered heading back home and slipping back into her bed, but then she remembered Alice's galactic eyes. The owner of those eyes couldn't have evil intentions. She didn't mind helping her out with her driving if she could. Karan hadn't driven since the accident, but Alice didn't know that and apparently didn't care. She knew she would not be able to get in the water, but maybe just being near a pool would be a good step toward healing this terrible fear.

She heard a distant rumble and looked toward the black skies for thunder clouds. It was cold enough to snow, so thunder was unlikely. Then she realized it was a car. It must be some local hoodlums, she thought, blitzed out of their minds, driving a low-rider home from a backwoods party somewhere.

The car turned out to be a classic Mustang, and it was the only car on the road for miles. It turned right in to the restaurant's gravel parking lot and stopped in front of where Karan sat on her log.

"Hey, Karan." Alice leaned out the window.

"How did you know my name?"

"You said it to that little man at the restaurant: with 'an' instead of 'en,' right?"

"Oh, I guess I did. What an idiot. Hey, I

thought you couldn't drive alone," Karan said, standing up from her log, but not sure if she should get in this car with this girl.

Alice rolled her eyes and looked like she regretted coming. "You coming or not?" she asked impatiently.

Karan walked around to the passenger door, and paused again. It was just a car door, but it felt like she was preparing to open a portal to another world, or another life. She looked at the old, dull brown paint that contrasted sharply with the shining hot-rod interior full of gadgets that, when pushed and prodded, probably made the car go much too fast.

She opened the door and got in.

Alice put it into gear and hit the gas. She didn't need to touch any of the fancy buttons because the car already knew how to hit Mach one without them. Karan scrambled for her seat belt and was pleased to discover a modern shoulder belt had been installed. In fact most of the inside of the car looked brand new.

"Where are you taking me?" she asked.

Alice glanced at her strangely. "Didn't you say you wanted to learn how to swim? Or did you lose your memory of last night's conversation too?"

"No, I mean how far away is your pool?"

Alice didn't answer, just drove down the highway out their little town of Golden toward Denver.

Karan watched the dry, empty hills roll by as they proceeded out of town and then south east into the first fancy housing developments on the edge of Denver.

The sky was starless and moonless, and there was a cold mist in the air that seeped its way into the car through a crack in Alice's window.

"Breakfast?" Alice asked, offering Karan a plastic jug that was about a foot high, full of some kind of green sludge.

"What is it?"

"I don't know. I usually eat leftovers from dinner, but Mom has me on some kind of health kick. I think it's raw kale, and some nasty raw protein powder. I put in a quart of ice cream to make it taste bearable."

"No thanks." Shivering in her sweatshirt, Karan folded her arms, protecting her scarred chest. She began to notice how thin she was— and vulnerable.

She looked over at Alice and noticed that she was completely relaxed. Her left hand dangled down from the steering wheel, her right hand held onto the two or three pound drink like it was just a popsicle. She didn't seem to notice the cold, even though she wore only a t-shirt and shorts.

After a twenty-minute drive, Alice finished her enormous green gloop drink just as they pulled into a very modern-looking bunch of domed buildings. Alice reverse-parked the car into a spot. Alice's parking job was fairly clumsily executed, Karan thought, but she didn't dare comment.

"Come on." Alice rolled up her window and got out.

Karan followed her around to the trunk.

Alice grabbed a bag, locked up the car, and walked toward the doors of the biggest dome.

Karan followed. Lettering announced the place was "Carmody Recreation Center."

A blast of heat and humidity hit them as they went in. Alice paid for them both.

Karan looked past reception and froze when she saw the huge expanse of water. It wasn't just a pool; it was like an indoor ocean. She knew if she got in that pool, she would drown. It was terrifying to be this close to certain death, and yet for reasons she didn't know, the chlorine smell was comforting and helped take some of the edge off her terror.

Dulling it enough, at least, that Karan could shuffle one foot in front of the other, rather than run back out to the car.

Alice looked back over her shoulder, saw that Karan was dithering, walked back and grabbed her firmly by the arm. They walked by the pool like that, Alice pulling and Karan trying to avoid looking at the water.

Karan could hear the rhythmic, gentle splashing noises that must have been swimmers doing laps. She heard the low, loud voice of a man giving instructions. He must be a coach, she thought, still without daring to look. It all sounded very serious and Karan knew she would need to run away at the first opportunity.

Alice pulled her into the women's change room and finally let go.

"I'm s-sorry," Karan stuttered, "but I can't go in the water 'cause I forgot a swim suit."

Alice threw her something from her bag.

"This is my mom's. She's pregnant so she won't be using it for a while. I bet it won't fit you well, but it will do. Nobody will see you anyway."

Something within Karan welled up when she touched the black Lycra suit that she held in her hand. It wasn't fear. It was a feeling of recognition, as though she was touching a well-loved relic. It felt almost like she had worn this very suit before, though she knew that was impossible, as she had never donned a swimsuit before in her life. It felt natural to strip down and step into it, so she did.

She caught Alice staring at the huge scar that sliced across one of Karan's reconstructed breasts, so she quickly pulled the straps over her shoulders. Her scar peeked out over the top, but otherwise the suit fit perfectly.

Alice quickly changed, and Karan noticed that her body, previously hidden by unbecoming athletic wear, was enormously strong, like that of a man—or a male athlete. She carried a lot of body fat and her muscles didn't look cut like those of a bodybuilder, but she was as strong as one. She had very long limbs that hung down, relaxed and bulky, from her body. Her shoulders were broad and her hips were narrow. Her breasts were small and she unceremoniously stuffed what was there into her suit, shouldered her bag and walked out toward the pool.

"Ready?" Alice asked without looking back.

"No," Karan said to the empty space. Karan took her clothes under her arm and reluctantly made her feet move forward after Alice. This time she had to actually look at the pool just to make sure she didn't accidentally fall in. She noticed that four of the pool's lanes were occupied by a team of men and women swimming steadily up and down the pool under the watchful eye of a man in a white golf shirt.

He looked at Karan as she emerged and did a double-take.

She wondered if he was looking at her scars or if he just knew she shouldn't be there. Not at 5:20 AM, not at this huge pool, and not with all these elite swimmers.

Alice ignored the coach, and his swimmers, and walked toward one of the unoccupied lanes. It had a sandwich board in front of it that read "fast lane."

Alice threw her bag down on a nearby bench and pulled out two caps and two pairs of goggles, handing one of each to Karan.

Karan had no idea what to do with them, so she copied Alice as she stretched the cap over her head and tucked her hair in, then stretched the goggles over the cap and fit them onto her eyes.

Karan was having trouble breathing because of her growing sense of dread. She knew no matter what happened, she was not getting into the water. It was enough that she came here, and Alice would just have to understand she had already taken a huge step by doing so.

Alice looked at her again.

Even though they both had blue goggles on, Karan could see that Alice's eyes were shining and iridescent. They were not kind eyes, but also not aggressive. As she wondered again who this strange girl really was, Alice walked over quickly behind Karan, took hold of her arms, pinned them to her sides, and lifted her off the ground.

Karan couldn't even scream, such was her terror, as Alice carried her over to the side of the pool.

"Just remember," Alice said from behind her, "blow bubbles, and kick, kick, kick."

It sounded oddly like the instructions you'd give a two-year-old, Karan thought, as Alice tossed Karan's full body length out over the water.

Time slowed down for Karan as some forgotten, deeply-held instinct kicked in. She jackknifed her body so she could enter the water head first, arms out front of her head, one hand folded over the other. Her hands broke the water surface first. She tucked her chin toward her chest and her head followed. She felt a pinch in her rehab chest muscles as she worked them in an unfamiliar way, following with a ripple through her stomach muscles and then a strong kick with both legs together that cascaded from hips down to toes. She did all this without thinking.

She was moving rapidly underwater, following a black line, and she propelled herself faster with two more kicks and then allowed herself to surface, still moving forwards at speed, feeling the water moving under her stomach. Rather than lift her head to breathe, she kept her head down and began to move her arms in loose, alternating arcs, her legs fluttering in powerful little kicks.

She didn't know if she was learning this for the first time or if it was coming from somewhere beyond her destroyed memory, but she loved it.

Her lungs began to crave oxygen and it occurred to her she had no idea how to breathe without stopping altogether. Just as that thought came, she rolled her head gently to the left and took a little breath, her mouth barely surfacing above the water near her left shoulder, and then she drew her face back down. Her arms never lost their rhythm. Now that she knew that her instincts had shown her she could breathe while swimming, she relaxed into a slower rhythm and reveled in the feelings of the water against her skin . Her hands and forearms were continuously learning how to find better purchase in the water and her abdominal muscles were holding her upper body firmly in connection with her legs.

She breathed left again and pushed her speed a little into the next few strokes, then breathed right and eased off.

She suddenly felt a fierce grip on her ankle, which stopped her dead in the water. She gasped, kicked her foot loose, and desperately searched for the bottom of the pool. Thankfully it wasn't deep and she was able to stand. Turning, she came face to face with Alice.

"Who *are* you?" Alice asked in a voice as firm and fierce as her grip on Karan's foot had been seconds earlier.

Karan was in too much rapture to be frightened by Alice's ominous tone.

They both lifted their goggles.

"Isn't it wonderful?" Karan said exultantly, a big smile spread across her scarred face. "I had no idea…"

"Cut it out. Come on, that was ridiculous. You swim better than I do. You swim better than anyone on that elite team over there."

"I do? But that's impossible. Today is my first swim ever. My dad said I never learned how to swim because of my aquaphobia."

"He's lying. I know what I'm talking about. Your stroke is the result of years of work. At least four hours a day in the water for years and years. You swim like someone who has lived and breathed swimming her whole life."

Karan looked over at the swimmers in the squad lanes and wondered if she really had been one of them before her accident.

She looked back at Alice. "Maybe," she said, putting the goggles back on, "some more swimming will help jog my memory."

Karan didn't really think she was going to regain her memory by swimming, but she also knew this conversation wasn't helping and she desperately wanted to return to the beautiful feeling of slicing through the water.

"Okay," Alice said, a strange look on her face, "let's do some laps. But you follow me this time. Do what I do."

"I'll try," Karan said, disappointed. All she

wanted to do was swim freely and feel the water against her body, but it was hard to say no to Alice.

To Karan's relief, Alice didn't go sprinting off down the pool. She swam slowly, relaxed, just as Karan had been doing. When the wall approached, Karan saw Alice flip herself around underwater and push off, and somehow Karan's body knew how to flip-turn just like Alice had.

She followed Alice up and down the pool like this for a while. She didn't count the laps and concentrated on following Alice's bubbles, and staying just close enough to make sure she kept up, but not too close. Karan focused on the explosions of information coming to her as her body continued to fine-tune it's conjugal connection with the water.

After ten minutes, she realized she was beginning to hurt. Her damaged chest muscles had responded well at first, but now they were beginning to ache, and her right shoulder was pinching.

Fortunately, Alice finally stopped at the wall and Karan pulled up next to her.

Thank God that is over, Karan thought, looking forward to a warm shower.

"Okay," Alice said. "That was a one

kilometer warmup. You kept up okay. Let's do some sets."

"What?" Karan asked. "We're not done?"

Alice finally smiled for the first time since they arrived at the pool: the first time since they'd met.

"I need to see what training you have had. We're going to do some IMs: individual medleys. You know what that is?"

"No idea: sounds pretty."

"Pretty hard: Butterfly, backstroke, breaststroke, freestyle," Alice said.

Something about those words clicked for Karan and she guessed her body would know what to do when the time came to do it.

"What you were just doing is freestyle, okay? But I guess you already know that, because you have the most beautiful freestyle technique I have ever seen, which means that you will have mastered all the other strokes too, and you're probably laughing at me inside."

"I'm not laughing at you inside."

"We'll do sets of four hundred meter IMs," Alice continued. "That's two laps of each stroke. I'm not going to worry about the clock for now. I'll swim behind you for the first one, so I can watch your stroke. Okay, go."

Karan's head was swimming with all that information, and she hoped her instincts would take over again. Before pushing off the wall to start whatever butterfly stroke was going to be, she looked back at the elite team and saw the coach was squatting at the edge of the water, speaking with one of the swimmers, and both were looking at her intently.

"Hear me?" Alice said. "Take off. This isn't a splash and giggle session anymore."

Karan did as she was told and pushed off the wall, aiming herself deep underwater. Again, her body did seem to know what butterfly meant, even though she had no memory of swimming like it before. It turned out butterfly involved strong, dolphin-like kicks that projected her upper body above the water, a deep breath followed by large powerful arcs with both of her arms together, her thumbs entering the water first, and then a big push with bent arms, all the way through to her hips. It felt great on her sore chest muscles and allowed her entire upper body to stretch out and rejuvenate. She was, however, exhausted by the end of the second lap and relieved to relax into a casual backstroke, which was like freestyle on her back. Following those two laps, breaststroke was the easiest and most relaxing of any of the disciplines she had tried yet. She wondered why they didn't call it frogstroke because the kick was frog-like, launching her into a long glide before she pulled her head and chest up with a strong motion with her arms, breathed, and frog-kicked again. Freestyle felt fantastic after loosening up her body with the other strokes. When she turned and began her last lap, the kinks were gone from her chest and shoulder and she knew Alice was right behind her, so she put on a playful little sprint to the wall, just for fun.

She pulled the goggles off and noticed the coach was staring at them again and looking at something on his phone.

"Okay, smarty pants," Alice said after reaching the wall and catching her breath. Then she seemed to smile a little again. "It's business time. Get out of the water and stand in front of the next lane. We're going to dive in this time and I'm going to race you."

"Hey, I'm really sorry. I didn't mean…"

"I'm not upset. I just want to try some race-pace sets. Just freestyle: four laps of the pool. Fast as you can. We'll see what kind of times you can do."

Karan obeyed, though she put on a pouty

face, which she thought probably looked strange with her scars. In any event she didn't mind going all out, if only just to see how it felt.

It felt amazing. Alice was incredible to swim against. Karan watched her underwater in the next lane and was inspired and immeasurably impressed by her style and strength.

In spite of Alice's superior strength and size, Karan kept up with her for two laps. Then everything collapsed for her. First her legs and abdominal muscles gave up, ruining the grace of her stroke, and even though she bravely kept splashing along after Alice, using only the failing strength of her arms, and dragging her immobile legs behind, there suddenly was a knife-like pain in her shoulder and she had to stop swimming altogether and stand up in the middle of the pool.

She felt like she couldn't even stand up or keep her head above water.

Alice seemed to have seen the whole thing and quickly came to Karan's aid.

"I got ya," she said, sliding a meaty arm under Karan's chest and pulling her toward the wall.

Karan could still see, but she felt like she

was surrounded by fire and there was nothing but fire to breathe, which was burning the remaining oxygen in her lungs.

The next thing she knew, she was waking up, lying on the concrete pool deck, staring up at a man in a white golf shirt.

"She's coming around," he said to someone behind Karan's head.

"I can see that," another voice said: Alice's voice.

Karan quickly sat up. Alice was behind her. "I'm so sorry, Alice. I don't know what happened."

"No, I'm sorry," Alice said. "I shouldn't have pushed you so hard."

"Who is she?" the man asked Alice.

"Don't worry about it," Alice said.

"She swims beautifully," he said. "I haven't seen a stroke like that since Katie Fremantle."

"Good thing she's not Katie." It was a girl's voice this time. "The spoiled brat; I wouldn't be caught dead in the same pool as her."

Karan lifted herself onto her elbows. The voice was coming from the edge of the pool where five of the elite swimmers were bobbing, goggles on their foreheads.

"I'm glad you're okay," another girl said. "We saw you get pulled out of the water."

"I'm fine," Karan said, embarrassed. "Sorry you guys had to stop training."

"I pass out sometimes when coach pushes us before a taper," the first girl said.

Karan didn't know what she was talking about, so she didn't respond.

"You guys training for nationals too?" one of the other girls asked.

Karan could only guess she meant the national swimming championships. Surely she was just kidding, she thought. Alice, maybe, but today was my first day in the water. Wasn't it?

"Nope," Karan said. "Just…a splash and giggle."

"Come join us this afternoon," the coach said. "It would be good for some of the girls to swim with you."

Karan was lost for words again, and when she turned to appeal to Alice for help, she saw she had already walked away. She tried to get up and follow her. The coach quickly reached down to help. She saw Alice had taken off her cap and was heading toward her bag and the locker room.

As she walked along the edge of the pool,

hearing the slap of her feet along the tiles, Karan noticed she was no longer afraid of the water at all. On the contrary, she felt like she belonged there.

She caught up with Alice in the showers. Karan didn't really know what to say and Alice had completely clammed up. After changing, they walked along in silence and left the building to a wash of cool air. It was still dark outside.

Without a word passing between them, they got in the car and Alice fired up the huge engine. They roared away from the pool at speeds Karan figured were a little excessive.

Karan decided not to push any conversation. She looked at the brightly lit, empty four-lane road. She looked at the massive two-story cookie-cutter houses they were passing. She wondered if she used to know anyone who lived in them.

As they drove up the ramp onto the C470 highway, Karan looked to her right and saw the sun rising over the small patch of high-rise buildings in the distance. There was a glint of yellow and pink on the glass-and-steel top of the tallest building. She knew that was downtown Denver because the hospital in which she had spent so much time these past six months was near downtown Denver somewhere.

The highway ended and split into a smaller one that ran either east toward the city of Denver or west toward somewhere called Boulder. They followed the westward way, entering the little town of Golden where Karan and her dad had moved after the accident.

Alice pulled into the parking lot for the riverside restaurant and stopped.

"Now what?" Karan asked. She was almost more bewildered by Alice's silence than she was by the realization that she had turned out to be a good swimmer.

Alice didn't say anything.

"Alice? Are you okay?"

At that moment Alice seemed to realize Karan was speaking to her.

"Yeah. Sorry."

"What happened back there?"

"You forgot what just happened?"

"No, Alice, I mean what happened to you."

"To *me*? You say you can't swim, then you swim like that, and you are asking what happened to *me*?"

"What happened to you after we swam?" Karan persisted. "Why did you leave so suddenly?"

Alice didn't answer for a while, but she turned off the motor, so Karan sat there and waited.

"I'm a little bit uncomfortable around some people: most people."

"You mean it wasn't because I passed out and almost drowned?"

"Kind of. No. I don't know." Alice squirmed a little in the driver's seat. She turned all the way toward Karan and leveled her mesmerizing eyes at her.

"So, *Karan,*" Alice continued with something of her earlier confidence.

Karan wasn't sure why she sounded like she was mocking her name.

"What do you know about your amnesia? You can't remember spending most of your previous life in a pool, but do you remember things like where you were born?"

"No idea where I was born. Mom died a long time ago. Dad said we relocated to Golden after the accident, so that I could be near my doctors. My driver's license is a Colorado one."

"What did he tell you about your car accident?"

"We were driving somewhere in the mountains. He was behind the wheel and he lost control and crashed into a rock. They had to airlift me to Denver."

"You crashed into a rock? Not water?"

"Nope. We hit a rock."

"He was okay?"

"I think so. He seems fine."

"And what about Facebook and all that?" Alice asked. "Did you check your profile? Maybe something from before the accident will jog your memory?"

"I apparently didn't do any social media," Karan said. "At least that's what Dad said."

"Seriously?" Alice asked, looking at Karan. "I thought I was the only one on the planet that didn't."

"Guess not."

"Do you have any family photos at home?"

"Lots: taken before my face was destroyed. They're all just pictures of me and my dad."

"Any friends?"

"I don't think so. Nobody has been in touch, anyway." "How about you?" Karan asked. "Where are all your friends?"

"I have a few back home. Hardrock is a mountain town about three hours' drive from here."

"You said your mom is with you and she's pregnant. What about your dad?"

"Back home."

"Brothers and sisters? Besides the new one on the way?"

"Brother. Dead. So have you tried meditation?"

"Oh my god, Alice, I'm sorry."

"Forget it. It was a long time ago."

"How do you get over something like that?"

"You don't. I just recently learned that I pretty much blocked it all out. It turned me into somebody that...they all thought I had a 'condition.' It made people avoid me. So I guess I kind of avoided them too."

"You mean you had something like amnesia too?"

"I guess."

"What helped you remember?"

"It's complicated. When I used to feel bad, I had this thing I would do. It didn't help me remember anything at first, but it made me feel better. And it made me be able to do a few things that others can't. I think it also made people think I was even weirder."

"You mean it helped you remember in the end? What did you do?"

"I just closed my eyes and relaxed, and concentrated on my breathing. There's more to it, but that's the main idea. My mom does it for a couple hours every day. I eventually found out what I was doing is called meditation. She's a yoga teacher and used to be in a cult in India where they meditated all the time."

Karan thought about that, and looked out the window at the embankment that led down to the river. The idea of water was giving her a bad feeling. Her swimming ecstasy was wearing off.

"Hey, I gotta go, Karan."

"Okay." Karan felt empty.

Alice appeared to notice Karan's sudden malaise and added, "I'm going to call around and see if I can figure out which swimming squad around here has been missing a girl for the last six months."

"Oh."

They were silent for a second. Karan didn't feel like she had the energy to get out of the car, let alone walk home.

"You don't look well. Can I just drop you at home?" Alice asked. "Maybe your dad won't care you've been out. And I could log a few more minutes of supervised driving."

"No way. Dad is really jumpy and he keeps a gun near the door. This car would scare the shit out of him."

"Wow."

As Karan sat there staring at the dashboard, she realized she couldn't possibly walk all the way home. She could hardly rouse herself to get out of the car.

"Actually, Alice, I think I'll take you up on that. We live up on a mountain. It's called Lookout Mountain."

"Yeah, I know the area. Nice."

"Can you just drive me part of the way up and I'll walk the rest of the way? If Dad's awake, I can just say I went for a walk."

"Sure," Alice said, starting the car and pulling out of the parking lot.

As they drove toward Lookout Mountain, Alice turned to Karan with a strange look on her face.

"Hey, what does your dad do anyway?"

"He drives people around all night for Uber. It's like a taxi service thing."

"I know about it. How can he afford a house on Lookout Mountain if he's a taxi driver?"

"I don't think he always was. I don't actually know."

As they wound their way up Lookout Mountain road, passing a few morning cyclists,

Alice gave Karan a few more meditation instructions. It seemed easy enough.

Karan was feeling better, and asked Alice to pull off at a little parking lot that had a viewing deck facing west. She could walk the rest of the way. They made an appointment to swim again in the afternoon and Alice left without saying goodbye.

What a strange girl, Karan thought.

At home, she snuck in quietly and found her dad was still asleep, so she went to her room and tried to meditate.

Alice's first instruction was to sit down on some pillows with her back against a wall, close her eyes, and relax deeply.

As soon as Karan propped herself up and closed her eyes, she could think of nothing besides the feeling of water. She relived the feeling of sliding through the water with skills innately remembered by her body, but not by her mind. She felt a rush of adrenaline as she remembered the brief race against Alice before she collapsed, and after she was revived, she recalled the other girls actually asking her if she was training for the nationals.

Alice was right. Meditation didn't make her remember anything about her past, but she felt better.

She got up off the floor, grabbed her pillows and lay down on the bed, giving in to the memories of her morning swim.

The next thing Karan knew, she was waking up to the sound of a text message arriving.

CHAPTER 3

Karan rolled over and picked up her phone to read the text message. She had never received one before from anyone besides her dad and a few doctors.

"Meet me at the Mayhem Gulch parking lot up Clear Creek Canyon in a half an hour. I'm organizing a picnic and I have some information about your dad. Don't tell him where you are going. He isn't who he says he is. - Alice"

Karan didn't remember giving Alice her number. Hoping to ask her for a lift, she dialed the number from which the message had been sent, but it rang out, with no voicemail.

She looked up Mayhem Gulch on some maps on her phone and found it was about ten miles west of Golden. It was eleven-thirty. She had no car. Alice would know that, wouldn't she, Karan speculated. It would take three or four hours to walk up there, or at least two hours to run, and she was not a runner—at least as far as she knew.

She tossed her phone down and rolled onto her back, wondering.

What could Alice have meant when she wrote that her dad wasn't who he said he was? Maybe she found out Dad wasn't an Uber driver? Maybe he was some kind of criminal, or a spy. Maybe he went around killing terrorists at night. She smiled at her own joke. She knew her Dad was harmless, but even if he wasn't an Uber driver, why would he care if she knew she used to be a swimmer before the accident? What kind of jobs had she done before the accident? Her dad had told her that she had been studying at a university. What if that was wrong too? Why was he lying about anything at all?

She thought about the terrifying scene she had hallucinated when she passed out at the restaurant. She had been injured and drowning, with a dead man on her, when her dad had rescued her. She wondered how much of that was based on a real, albeit fragmented memory of the accident.

The same feeling of emptiness and exhaustion she experienced at the restaurant swept over her again. She felt like her heart and her guts had all been gouged out and replaced with brackish water.

She tried meditating again, but she was too agitated to even close her eyes.

Her eyes fell on a photo on her bedside table. It was a little framed shot of her and her dad. It could have been two years old or ten years old. She had no way of knowing how her face had grown and aged before it was destroyed and required all that plastic surgery. Dad looked about the same as he does now. She wished she could feel something toward him: remember all the tender moments they must have had. She looked really happy in the photo.

She picked it up, turned it over and saw the price tag was still on the frame. It was dated in the current year, which was weird because it looked like an old photo. Dad must have got it reframed recently, she thought, but she was still curious. She unclipped the frame backing so she could pull out the photo. It was dated this past November, the same month of her accident. Now that was very strange. He must have had it reprinted so that she would have something familiar on her bedside table.

Right?

Her gaze raced around the room and her body followed, jumping up to take down two different photos that were hanging on the wall.

Both had the same dates on the frames and photos.

They were all props and this was a stage.

Karan's feeling of emptiness suddenly flushed away, replaced by abject horror.

She heard something downstairs and knew her dad was down there, probably making his coffee.

Karan grabbed her phone and charger, her wallet, put her running shoes back on, and very quietly opened her bedroom window. Her heart was beating so hard it felt like it could rip through the scars on her chest.

Uber.

She pulled out her phone, downloaded the Uber app, and tried to get it all working so she could order a getaway car, but she didn't have a credit card—no PayPal account, nothing—so she failed to order a car. Her dad always said, with pride, that taxis took much longer than

Uber cars up here. She didn't think she could wait that long.

Pocketing her phone, she climbed out the window and tiptoed down the thin asphalt shingles until she reached the rain gutter. She peered over it and down at an eight or nine foot drop into a hedge. It was nice and bushy, though it was an evergreen and not likely as soft as it looked.

Wondering if she might be able to turn around and hang down from the rain gutter, she put her foot on it to test its strength. The gutter bent easily down, making a metallic creak. There was no way it would hold her weight.

She thought about what the man inside was doing. She hesitated. Was it possible that she was wrong about him? That he *was* her dad, rather than some stranger, or kidnapper, or worse. She had no memory and little information, so she closed her eyes, breathed, and tried to examine her feelings.

She was absolutely sure now that she felt nothing for him—nothing but fear.

Karan turned and jumped off the roof.

The landing was worse than she'd imagined. Not only was the hedge not soft, it was full of sharp, unyielding branches that cut into both her legs through her clothes. One of her ankles had twisted underneath her as well, which meant she probably couldn't walk very far.

She remained still, accepted the pain in her body, closed her eyes and listened for any sound from the house. After nearly a minute of this, she'd heard nothing. She found herself going through the first steps of Alice's meditation again. Breathe deeply, relax the body; let the thoughts come and go like passing clouds. Her only thoughts right now concerned the six-month-old photos in her bedroom, put there by the strange man inside the house who called himself her father. Accept the thoughts, she told herself. Let them go. Breathe.

Somehow this process started to guide her away from the pain in her legs and ankle and she found a place within her that was quiet and Dad-less.

Inside the quiet of that space was an image of Alice, walking away from her, full of strength and purpose. Alice was rough, but she seemed to mean well, when she could be bothered, and she was the only person in her life Karan could trust. Alice was the only person in her life, period.

Karan opened her eyes and knew exactly what she was going to do.

She gingerly disentangled herself from the hedge, which would never be the same again, and walked away from the front door toward the garage.

Opening the door was the impossible hurdle. She again thought of Alice and began to open it, so slowly it took nearly five full minutes. Aside from a few tiny squeaks, it remained silent enough.

She found not-Dad's keys hanging on a hook on the wall behind a jacket and then did the same slow routine with the car door. It took her five painstaking minutes until she was finally sitting in her not-Dad's Toyota, key in the ignition, no clue how to drive a car.

She knew she could not let him hear her, which meant she couldn't turn on the engine yet. She closed her eyes and tried to recall the steps her not-Dad had routinely taken when he sat down behind the wheel.

She listened again for any sounds from the house. Hearing none, Karan opened her eyes and turned the keys until the car electrics switched on, but not the engine. She quickly turned the radio off before it made any sound. As they had in the pool, her hands were beginning to guide her based purely on her muscles' own memories. She put the car into neutral gear and took the emergency brake off. Nothing happened because the car was parked on a flat space. She slowly, slowly opened the car door again and placed her foot on the ground, pushing as hard as she could. The car only rocked a few inches.

Karan got out of the car and stood next to it, placing both hands on the back of the driver's side door frame. Leaning into it with all her strength, pushing off on her one good leg, she managed to get the car rolling, and then dove into it at the last moment, putting her foot on the brake.

The brakes betrayed her with a screaming, dry, squeaking noise, and she knew there was nothing to do but get the hell out of there.

She stopped the car completely. Her hands knew to put it in park before turning the ignition. The engine fired right up and she was putting it into reverse when the man she used to think was her dad came running out the front door with a look of panic on his face.

As she jammed it into reverse and stepped on the gas, she looked at him again and saw his panic appeared genuine. It was a look worse than panic, a look like he was staring down the throat of an unfathomable tragedy. She almost felt bad for him as she screeched the brakes, flipped the shifter into D, passed it and accidentally put it into "1", which seemed to work well enough, and sped off.

The man she used to call Dad chased her for a while, screaming, "Karan!" Her last image of him in the rear-view mirror burned itself into her memory. He was bending over, his hands on his knees, and it looked like he was sobbing.

She recognized that look. It was exactly how she felt. Bereft. Alone.

Even through her own sobs, thankfully she drove well enough, at least after she managed to get the car into D. She followed the road back down into Golden, ignoring the calls that began to start coming in from not-Dad. She followed Highway 6 out of town, up into Clear Creek Canyon, and started the drive toward her rendezvous with Alice.

As she snaked up through the valley, sparsely-wooded hills rising up on both sides of the road and a roaring river running always within view, emotional waves washed over her, alternating between relief, horror, self-doubt, and determination, in that order. Relief to be putting distance between herself and the man who was most certainly lying to her about who she was; horror that she had no idea who she was before the accident, nor why he had surrounded her with stage props; self-doubt arising from the image of him broken and bawling in her rear-view mirror; and finally, determination to catch up with Alice, the only one on the planet she felt like she could trust right now.

After ten minutes, she finally found the turnoff for Mayhem Gulch and pulled off into the parking lot. There was a little hut containing public toilets, a trailhead, and a half dozen parked cars. The trailhead led left from the parking lot and switch-backed up a bald hill. To the right of the trailhead was a dry creek bed. Following it up with her eyes, she saw it ended in a series of dramatic black cliffs.

Thankfully Alice's car was there in the parking lot.

Karan pulled out her phone. It was just past twelve noon. She slowly pulled into a parking spot a few cars down from the Mustang. She figured Alice would either be waiting for her in the car or maybe would be sitting in the shade under one of the trees near the trailhead. Karan got out, stretching her muscles, tired from her escape and from the swim that morning. She limped over to the Mustang.

At first the glare prevented her from seeing him. Karan was right next to the driver's side before it became apparent it was not Alice in the car. It was the skinny guy from the bar last night.

She turned to run but knew it was hopeless. Her injured ankle carried her only ten feet before she tripped and slid into the dirt, cutting her hands on the gravel.

"Whoah!" His unnaturally deep voice sounded behind her. "Take it easy."

"Touch me and I'll scream."

"I'm not going to touch you, sweetheart: just here to help. Your friend Alice asked me to wait here for you."

"Not likely," Karan said, rolling over so that she could face the man who was obviously hunting her. "It looked to me like she was knocking you on your ass last night."

"Looks can be deceiving. She didn't tell you I'm her uncle? She has a fiery temper, but she explained to me everything about your predicament; how you two went for swim this morning, and then she came to me for help in researching your background."

Karan didn't say anything and managed to

push herself painfully back into a standing position.

"Okay?" he continued in his soothing voice. "She said she invited you for a picnic, right?"

Karan didn't answer, but softened.

"Now she has made a little picnic for you down the road and told me to wait here and drive you over there when you arrive. She originally wanted to have it here, but there weren't any good picnic spots."

Karan looked around skeptically. It seemed like there were plenty of spots for a picnic. Would the Alice whom she knew even want to put out a nice picnic for someone? Wouldn't Alice probably rather sit on the hood of her car and eat cold pizza? Then again, how well did she really know Alice? She'd met her less than twenty-four hours ago.

"Shall we?" the skinny guy asked, smiling.

Her mind continued to race. How else would he have Alice's car? Or could he have stolen it? If so, where was Alice? Surely she would be up here somewhere, according to that text message. So he must be telling the truth because how else would he know Alice had taken Karan swimming and she was going to help delve into Karan's background?

Karan nodded and slowly walked toward Alice's car.

The guy seemed relaxed and led the way.

She followed, scanning the hills, and the trail that climbed up one of them, hoping for a glimpse of Alice.

They got in, and then it was too late.

He immediately grabbed Karan's left hand and zip-tied it to a bike-lock attached to something under the dashboard. Then he reached over her and pulled her seat belt on, connecting the buckle with a little click.

She looked around her in a fit of panic and saw a dozen mobile phones on suction cup mounts all over the car's dashboard and rear window. Some of them were facing inward, some facing outward. As far as she could tell, they were all on, recording or transmitting something.

Karan was beyond screaming, so she just closed her eyes and tried to breathe.

"We're not going to hurt you, Karan," he said to her. It sounded like he was speaking to her underwater. "I promise. Just relax. I had to restrain you so you wouldn't panic. Listen to me," he said when Karan didn't open her eyes. "Your friend Alice is not who you think she is. She's extremely dangerous, and I'm taking you somewhere that you will find extremely interesting. I'm trying to help."

Karan's eyes snapped open and she searched the terrain outside of the car again, looking for Alice. She hoped she was somewhere around here, but she couldn't see her anywhere.

The skinny guy had pulled the Mustang out of its parking spot and stopped in the middle of the parking lot, facing toward the highway, engine idling angrily. Karan could see the Mayhem Gulch trailhead and her eyes followed it up the hill, where it crept out of view. She looked to the right at the dark layers of cliffs. The highest ledge was about five hundred feet away. Standing there was a lone figure, facing her direction.

Her captor woke up one of the phones mounted on the dashboard, the only one that didn't seem to be on. He opened a video-calling application and touched a contact. The line immediately connected and Alice's face was there, livid, jaw set with angry facial muscles, her eyes no longer beautiful, but narrow and focused and weaponized.

"Karan, why did you invite me up to this cliff? And why are you trying to steal my car?"

"What?" Karan asked, and then realized

the phone was pointing only at her.

"I'm not stealing anything!" she shrieked. With her free right hand, she adjusted the phone to point at the skinny guy in the driver's seat. "I've been kidnaped by this asshole!"

"Okay, enough name-calling," her captor said, reaching up and killing the connection. They both turned and watched Alice.

Karan could just see Alice well enough in the distance to recognize she was putting her phone in her pants pocket. Then Alice did something inexplicable.

She dove straight off the cliff.

"Shit," the skinny guy intoned. He seemed to have seen what Karan just saw.

Karan kept her eyes glued on Alice. She was horrified she had caused the death of her new friend, but Alice didn't appear to be panicking in the air. She looked to be gracefully diving toward a soft landing.

Just when it looked like Alice was going to splatter straight into the black boulders at the bottom of the cliff, she began to move her body, almost like she was swimming.

Her fall was being arrested. Alice's body appeared to shrink into a point but then Karan realized it was an optical illusion. Alice had only leveled out and was swimming horizontally, directly toward the parking lot, gaining on them fast.

When the skinny guy saw that, he turned forward and pounded on the accelerator. The engine roared and the back wheels spun furiously in the gravel with no forward movement in the car.

The Mustang's rear tires finally found some purchase on the gravel parking lot and jerked forward toward the highway. Once on the asphalt, the back wheels fishtailed to the left before gaining traction. The car burst forward away from the parking lot, engine roaring, RPM screaming, gears changing.

Karan had no idea a car could go that fast. It was so physically overpowering for her, she couldn't process what was happening. All she could do was keep her eyes on Alice, who appeared to still be gaining on them in spite of their furious burst of speed.

Karan glanced at the skinny guy only once. He appeared to be scared. His mouth was hanging open and his eyes darted between the road in front of him and the rear-view mirror. He kept trying to push the car faster. They hit a curve too fast and almost careered into the guard rail, but the guy hit the gas hard and somehow the car pulled itself back onto the highway.

After thirty seconds, Alice was close enough that Karan could see her face. Then Karan couldn't see her anymore because she was above them.

Her captor got really worried and began taking even bigger risks in an effort to lose their angry, invisible pursuer.

A very loud smashing noise echoed above the roar of the engine and Karan saw two dents form in the roof of the car.

Alice's white fingers gripped onto Karan's window.

Karan heard Alice scream, "Karan, grab the steering wheel!"

The skinny guy jerked the wheel to the left in an effort to shake Alice off and the Mustang headed straight for the guardrail, the only thing between them and a precipice down to the raging river.

Karan lunged for the wheel with her right hand and managed to pull it a little toward her, just as she saw one of Alice's hands reach through the driver's side window. Alice grabbed the skinny guy's arm and pulled him completely out of the window. It was as though he had been sucked out of an airplane. He was gone and Karan was alone in a car that was careering toward an embankment.

She did the only thing she could think of, which was to jerk the wheel again. This simply turned the Mustang sideways and it slid into the guardrail at forty miles an hour, passing through it like it was made of butter. The car was suddenly silent as it flew sideways through the air. Karan had enough time to let go of the steering wheel and brace for impact. She glanced to her right and caught a glimpse of Alice and the skinny guy twenty feet up in the air.

Rather than an explosive jolt, the car landed on something soft and slid gracefully for two or three seconds. Karan breathed out, reached over and pulled the emergency hand brake, which did nothing. The car righted itself and Karan could see it was heading straight for the river.

They plunged into the river with the smash Karan had been expecting earlier. The impact brought her back into the scene she had hallucinated at the restaurant. It was more vivid this time. She was in the same car and her dad was next to her, his eyes closed: dead maybe. Water was rushing in through the broken windows and windscreen.

She was injured and heartbroken.

"What did he do to your hand?"

Alice's voice brought Karan back to the present moment. Water was coming into the car, but only at a trickle, and only through the bottom of the door that Alice had just opened. Karan's awareness slowly began to return. She could see the Mustang only had its front hood submerged in the river. It was a slow-moving section of water and she didn't seem in any danger of drowning.

"I've got a knife in the glove box," Alice said. "Just a sec."

Karan's hand was completely red, as though she was wearing a red ski glove. Curious, she thought.

She could see the bottom edge of the ski glove was actually a dent ending in something that looked like bone.

After Alice cut the plastic zip-tie and peeled the red plastic out of Karan's flesh, the pain hit her. It was unbelievable. She knew her hand was going to be damaged forever. It was completely dead.

Alice took off her shirt, wrapped it tightly around Karan's hand, and helped her out of the car.

Karan was surprised to be able to walk. She was floating. She knew she was in shock.

"Just sit down here, Karan," Alice said gently, indicating the river rocks near the Mustang. Karan could hear it ticking and hissing over the rush of the river.

"I'm going to go get that guy," Alice said.

Karan watched as Alice walked up the slope until she reached the prone figure. She picked him up and carried him over like a sack of potatoes.

Throwing him down next to Karan, Alice returned to the Mustang and found another couple of the skinny guy's zip ties. She zipped the guy's hands together tightly, then his feet. She opened up a container of water she had strapped to her lower back and emptied it onto his face.

He spluttered to consciousness and threw his hands in front of his face.

"We're not going to hurt you, asshole," Alice said, "unless you don't start explaining."

"I...how did you do that?" he stammered. "They said you were a freak but they didn't say you could do...that."

"Who?" Alice demanded.

"What the hell else can you do? Breathe fire?"

"If you don't tell me who sent you, I'm going to show you what else I can do."

"Hey, relax," he said, to himself as much as to Alice. Then he noticed Karan and her hand. "Oh, my god, I'm really sorry. I would never have taken this job if I thought either of you would get hurt. You're just kids, for God's sake."

"A job for who?" Alice asked.

"I do some jobs for this guy in Denver. He got in touch with some family from India. Some fancy family with lots of money."

"Names."

"They didn't tell me. I just had a handful of Skype contacts that are all gibberish."

"What did they want?"

"They paid me to set up a situation where you were on top of a cliff somewhere with no witnesses, and to give you a strong incentive to get to the bottom of it as fast as possible. I was supposed to video the whole thing and stream it to those Skype contacts."

Alice looked back at the Mustang and ran in to grab all the phones he had mounted in the car.

When she came back, Karan observed that the phones Alice held were still connected to video calls. The screens were, however, all black.

"Who are you?" Alice shouted at one of

the phones in her hand, but there was just silence. The lines stayed open, the screens an ominous black.

Alice went through the phones one by one and disconnected the calls, then put them in her swimming bag in the boot of her destroyed car. All but one.

Alice faced the skinny guy again. "Why?" she demanded.

"How am I supposed to know? All they said was they heard from some other Indian, who was in your town recently, that you are a freak. They wanted proof."

"Was it part of the job to smash my car and try to rip Karan's hand off?"

"No, no, no. They don't know about her—and they don't care. I just used her as the incentive and I..." turning to Karan again, he said, "I'm so, so sorry——"

"Focus, dude," Alice interrupted in an icy voice.

He gazed fearfully at Alice. "I had no idea you would...I still can't believe it. I thought you were just supposed to be some kind of really good climber, like a mountain goat or something. Nobody was supposed to get hurt, especially not her. I was just going to film your freak thing, whatever it was, and then take

Karan on a little drive to see something."

"See what?" Karan finally said, recovering enough to speak.

"I bugged Alice's car and heard you two talking about your amnesia and your dad. It sounded like your dad is not your dad. Obviously it all started when you had that accident. So I looked up your hospital records and found the Jeffco Police crash report."

"Isn't that all private?" Karan asked.

"Pah-lease," he said, apparently relaxing now that Karan was talking.

"And then what?" Alice asked.

"I went to the crash site this morning. The report described a single vehicle that broke through the guard rail and struck a boulder. The collision with the boulder prevented the vehicle from plunging down a steep embankment into the river, but resulted in your injuries."

"And?"

"And this morning I found something the police missed."

"Yeah, and you're some genius investigator."

"Sometimes the police just can't see things because they can't imagine the kinds of brutal, crazy things people can do to one another. I don't have that problem."

Alice didn't say anything.

"It was also probably because the river is running at much lower volume than it was six months ago. You will be interested to see it, Karan. I was going to take you there. It's just a little bit further up from here. That's why I set all this up to happen here, so that I could help you out."

Alice looked at Karan and then back at the guy.

"Then what?" Alice asked.

"Alice," Karan said, "don't listen to him. He's just trying to find a way to escape."

Alice looked at Karan and shook her head in a motion small enough that the skinny guy might not have noticed.

"Why did you want to help Karan find the crash site?" Alice asked him.

"I'm not a bad guy. I never take any jobs that involve hurting anyone. I have a family to support. Karan's story was just interesting and I suppose I also wanted to prove to you that I wasn't out to hurt either of you two."

"What are they paying you?"

He blew some air out of his mouth. "Not enough."

"Amount, dude."

"Ten grand."

"Is one of these your phone?" Alice said, holding up her swimming bag.

"Yep. The old beat-up one."

Alice dug around and found the right one, then looked at something else on the other phone she was holding.

"What's your name?"

"Bruce."

"Bruce what?"

"Why?"

"Okay, never mind. I don't care." Alice punched a few buttons on the phone she had been holding the whole time and then put it in her pocket. "Here's what you're gonna do, Bruce. I just videoed everything you just said: your whole confession. I bet most of it was bullshit, but some of it was probably true. I just put it in a message to my friend in the Hardrock police and I have it all ready to press send. If you don't want me to do that, here's the deal."

Karan looked over at the skinny guy. His eyes were big.

"First, you're going to keep your mouth shut about how I'm a freak. You'll never mention it to anyone. Not to your friend in Denver, not to his Indian friends, not to your friends at the bar, not to your wife or your kids, not to your parole officer, not to you priest. No-one. Ever."

He nodded.

"Second, it seems you know a bit about cars, seeing as how you just stole mine. So you're going to go check it out for me and tell me if it can be driven or not."

He snorted. "No way," he blurted. "That thing is gone——"

Alice held her phone up, ready to press the send button.

"Okay, okay. Check out your car. That's a ten-second car, by the way. Was. You probably didn't even know that."

"Whatever. Third, you're going to use your phone to transfer that ten thousand dollars to my bank account. I'm going to give it all to Karan to help her get back on her feet after all this."

Bruce looked like he wanted to open his mouth, but held the words back.

"Fourth. You're going to walk with us to Karan's crash site."

He nodded without hesitation.

"Lastly, you're going to tell me how to find your boss in Denver—and give me an introduction. I want to ask him about those

Indians."

"I can't do that. You don't ask these guys questions about anything or anyone——"

Alice pressed send. Bruce looked shocked. After a second, when it had fully registered, he sank into the ground, defeated.

They all sat in silence for a while. Karan was still unable to move her hand and it was starting to bleed through Alice's shirt.

Alice's phone rang.

"Hey, Nancy," Alice said, then listened. "Yeah, he's still here. What should I do with him?"

Another pause. "Okay. Thanks, Nancy." Alice hung up. "Cops and ambulance are on their way," Alice said gently to Karan. She was ignoring Bruce now that he was of no further use to them.

"Alice," Karan said. "I think I need to see that other crash site. If I get taken off in an ambulance, I have no idea when I'll get back here, and it's kind of urgent for me now."

"Why? Bruce here, if that's even his name, was just bullshitting about that."

"Maybe, but I kind of stole my Dad's car and almost ran over him when I blasted out of the garage. I'm pretty sure he's not my dad. but he's somebody, and I feel like I owe it to myself, and maybe to him, to figure out what's at that site."

"How far, Bruce?" Alice asked.

He didn't answer. He had laid back onto the gravel and was staring at the sky.

Alice looked around, and then at her car. She grabbed Bruce, hauled him to his feet, and dragged him, struggling, over to the Mustang. She shoved him in the passenger seat where Karan had been trapped before. Using another one of his zip ties, she hog-tied his hands and feet to the same bike lock he had used to bind Karan. This forced him into a position so awkward and tight that he let out a deep grunt like a pig.

"Let's go," Alice said to Karan. "You good to walk?"

"I think so."

CHAPTER 4

They walked upstream, feet crunching along the river rocks that lined the space between the road and Clear Creek, which was much bigger than a creek, Karan thought. Aside from the odd car on the road above them, they were completely alone.

Karan wondered why none of those cars bothered to stop at the place where Alice's Mustang had punched through the guardrail. Surely there were nasty skid marks and torn metal. If someone noticed, wouldn't they stop to peer over the edge and see if everything was okay?

She wondered if people demonstrated the

same indifference six months ago after her first crash.

Her ankle felt better now she was walking and Alice had fortified her with some ibuprofen and a couple of energy gels she had in her swimming bag. The bleeding in her hand was slowing, but she still held it tightly into her stomach in a protective gesture.

All they knew was Bruce found something in the river below the rock Karan's dad's car had crashed into. They carefully searched the bank below the road for any signs of disturbance.

As Bruce had said, the creek was running low, clear and fast, slowed only occasionally by a boulder in the middle creating a deep pool behind it. They examined a few of those slow pools from the side of the river, but nothing was suspicious.

After walking for about ten minutes, Karan thought she heard a distant siren. Alice looked up, but she continued walking.

Up ahead, Karan saw the river widened and was still, and beyond that it narrowed into a canyon that was going to be impassable for them. When they reached it, they would have to turn back. Maybe the police could help her figure it all out.

Alice had seen something and was striding purposefully ahead.

At first Karan didn't see it, but as she walked toward the wide, still section of water, she thought she knew what Alice had seen.

When they got closer, she was sure. There was an old landslide consisting of massive boulders that ran from the road above and spilled down to the creek, right before it narrowed into the canyon. On the near side of the landslide, there appeared to be something metallic shining between some of the smaller rocks that were submerged in the water.

Alice reached the site way ahead of Karan and started wading in the water near the landslide.

By the time Karan had caught up, Alice had walked around the site a few times and seemed to come to a conclusion.

"The collision with the boulder up top must have started a landslide into the river, which covered everything so that the police didn't see it."

"See what? What's down there, Alice?"

Alice just looked at her, started to speak, and then stopped—and then started again.

"Karan, you remember this morning when that swimming coach said you swam like Katie

Fremantle?"

"Yeah."

"And then that other girl said that she was glad you weren't Katie because Katie Fremantle's a spoiled brat?"

"Yeah."

"I think you're Katie Fremantle."

Karan didn't know what to say.

"Before I got your text today, that turned out to be from Bruce inviting me here for the trap, I called my swimming coach back in Hardrock and asked if he knew of any missing elite swimmers. He told me he heard Katie and her dad had stopped going to their pool in Arizona. Her dad was also her coach. A real jerk, apparently, and used to treat Katie like a machine, not a human. Always had. Six months ago, she was training for nationals, which she was expected to win in several disciplines, by the way, and she had some kind of breakdown. So her dad said she needed some time out and they left to go on a holiday, and didn't tell anyone where they were going."

Karan looked at the pile of boulders, then back at Alice. "And Katie's a spoiled brat? Who had a nervous breakdown?"

"I guess. But you're not a brat. Oh, and she's my age, not twenty-one. She's sixteen."

"What does she look like?"

"Not like you. But maybe like you before your nice new dad gave you all that plastic surgery. Want to see a picture from the internet?"

"No, I do not want to see." Karan said, and then fell to the ground, exhausted. The sirens were getting louder.

"Listen, whoever you are," Alice said with her usual lack of tact. "It may just be a total coincidence. We may never learn what really happened, but I at least want to go look at what's underwater here."

"You think there were two cars in the accident, not one, and my real dad is under those rocks."

"Maybe. Or it could be just some other car that crashed here some other time and nobody found it until now. There's definitely something under there and only one way to find out what it is."

Karan thought the sirens were now loud enough, that they must be arriving at the scene and would be trying to find them.

"Go, quick."

Alice kicked off her shoes and waded into the water.

Karan wondered how cold it was. Must be

freezing.

"Hey, be careful, Alice!" she shouted.

Alice ignored her and waded around the pile of rocks until she was standing in chest deep water. She was having trouble maintaining her footing and was gasping because of the cold.

She lost her footing and went under.

"Alice!" Karan yelled, getting up and rushing over to the water's edge.

"She's gone, Karan," a voice said from behind her.

Karan swiveled around and saw the man with whom she had been living for the past six months. She knew now he wasn't her father but she felt sorry for him. He was carrying his shotgun and was walking slowly down the scree toward her.

"Everything is gone, Karan."

"Dad," she said, trying to smile. "Thank God you're here!"

He stopped in his tracks, paused, and then continued walking.

"Enough of that Dad stuff. I know that you know."

"What are you talking about, Dad?" Karan feigned confusion.

"I knew you would figure it out someday,

but I hoped by then we would have developed a strong enough bond that it wouldn't matter. You found out the wrong way. I saw the look on your face and I knew."

Karan looked back at the creek and saw no sign of Alice.

"Look, Dad, we gotta help her. It's been a whole minute and the water is freezing cold. She's drowning down there!"

"I knew that woman would bring you here," he said, standing there looking at the water. "It's all her fault."

"Dad, the police are here looking for me, you know."

"That's probably just as well. My life is over—again."

Something caught Karan's peripheral attention but she didn't dare take her eyes off this man and his gun.

"Why did you bring your gun?"

He looked down, as if seeing it for the first time.

"I don't know," he finally said. He didn't take his finger off the trigger.

The strange thing was that Karan kept thinking about the devastated look he wore when she'd driven off a few hours ago. It had ignited the first real feelings she had felt toward him. She felt bad for him then and worse for him now. "I can see you're really suffering," she said, "and I'm really sorry."

"Suffering? You have no idea," he said.

Karan picked up the movement in the corner of her eye again. There was something moving on the boulders in the landslide about thirty feet above and behind her fake dad.

The figure sprang, and she could see it was Alice, arms and legs flailing. She flew through the air and landed right on the man's back, forcing his head to whip back.

Instantaneously a shot fired and Karan fell to the ground. The sound deafened her and felt like the rocks themselves had landed on her head. As she tried to feel where the shot had hit her, she heard the huge blast echoing up into the valley.

She looked up and saw Alice standing on the man, who looked like he wasn't going anywhere ever again.

"Yes, she does know suffering," Alice said. "She has forgotten more suffering than you have ever known."

CHAPTER 5

It took a minute or two before Karan realized the shot had missed her. She remained on the ground, Alice stayed on the guy, and the two girls stared at each other. Alice was dripping on the guy and Karan's ears were ringing.

It seemed like hours passed, when in reality it was only thirty seconds before the police rushed down the embankment, weapons raised.

Alice raised both her hands, but Karan couldn't raise either of hers. The police cuffed Alice and sat her down away from the unconscious man in the dirt.

"You'll find two bodies seat-belted in a car

under those rocks," Alice told them. "I saw them. I think one is Katie Fremantle's dad," she continued. "The other one is this jerk's daughter, Karan somebody. With an 'an' instead of 'en'."

One of the police officers looked skeptically down at the pile of rocks and then conferred with a colleague.

"You'll find you guys screwed up the investigation of a crash that happened here six months ago. There were two cars involved, not one. Since this guy lying on the ground couldn't have known the people in the other car, I'm guessing each car had one survivor. This guy survived in his car, while his twenty-one-year-old daughter, Karan, died next to him. My friend here with the bleeding hand is Katie. Her dad died in the crash and I don't know how she survived, but she did. The only thing I can think of is that this weirdo pulled himself together and went to her aid. He waded into the water, found the car under all those rocks, dove in and pulled Katie out of her car. Her face was smashed beyond recognition."

"That seems hardly possible," one of the police officers said. "I fly-fish here with my kid. This river is practically iced over in the winter."

"Oh," Alice said.

"No," another officer said, "that was November, so it probably wasn't that cold yet. It would have been about the same as it is now."

"Anyway," Alice said in an exasperated tone, "that's what happened, guys, and then the really weird stuff started."

Karan realized Alice was talking about her, and her real name was Katie. She was suddenly alert and clear, as though someone had just bilge-pumped the muck out of her head.

"Katie here must have still been conscious, and had hit her head and gotten amnesia. I'm guessing that when she was pulled from the car, she called him 'Dad,' or something like that, which overloaded his brain circuits and gave him a really stupid idea: stupid and gross. After he laid Katie down somewhere, he went back up to his smashed car, took his dead daughter out, strapped her into Katie's car underwater, and left them there for the trout to eat."

"Not plausible," the fly-fishing officer said. "Even if they didn't see the submerged car, the officers who took the call would have seen tire tracks and other evidence it had been a two-car collision."

"You'd think, huh?" Alice said. "Maybe Karan's dad knows someone in the police force. I don't know; I'm just a sixteen year old girl."

"You're a what?" Both officers squinted at Alice, disbelieving.

"Then it got even weirder." Alice was looking sad-eyed at Katie..

"When Katie woke up in the hospital," Alice continued, "and her doctors told her nice new dad that her amnesia was probably going to stick, and that she needed facial reconstruction, he gave them his real daughter Karan's photo to model her new face after. Then she really became his new Frankenstein daughter, Karan."

"No offense, Katie," Alice said quickly. "It's a figure of speech. I didn't mean you look like Frankenstein."

Alice paused and looked at the police officers, who had their mouths open.

"You guys got all that?" she asked angrily.

"Alice," Karan asked, tentatively, "what did they look like?"

"Who?"

"My dad and that girl under the water."

"You don't want to know. I don't want to know. I couldn't see clearly, thank God."

After Alice made a statement to the police, the ambulance finally showed up for Karan, who was trying to get used to the idea that her name was really Katie, and that she was supposed to be a spoiled brat.

She couldn't help watching them tend to Karan's father, who had woken up and appeared to be bent, but not broken.

She didn't get around to asking about Bruce, but she guessed he would have been taken into custody and charged with something, based on the confession Alice videoed and sent to the police.

CHAPTER 6

A few days later, Katie heard a knock on her hospital door. Alice peeked around the corner.

"How you doing, Katie?" she asked.

"As of this morning," she responded with a smile, "I can start to feel my fingers again. The doctor had a look and said the nerve damage was probably minimal, and so I should make a full recovery."

"Cool."

"So," Katie asked, "you still heading home this afternoon?"

"Yeah. My dad finished shifting all our stuff into the cabin we're moving into."

"Oh. You didn't say you're moving to a

cabin. That sounds cool. Is your car ready yet?"

"Nope. I'll have to come back down next week. They had to rebuild it again."

There was an awkward silence for a moment and then Alice reached into her bag.

"Here," she said.

Katie took the plastic bag from Alice, looked inside and saw a new pair of goggles, cap, and her mom's used Speedo swim suit.

"I figured this one fit you pretty well the other day, so…"

"Thanks, Alice. I love it."

Alice looked down at the ground for a while, like she wanted to turn and leave.

"Hey, Alice," Katie said. "I think I'm going to get a bunch of money out of this. My dad had a lot of assets and a house and everything. They can't find anyone else to give it to, and he, I mean we, didn't have any other close family."

"That's lucky. I mean that sucks."

"I guess. And the courts are going to have to try to locate some distant relative and give them custody of me, or maybe they'll put me in a foster home."

Katie was surprised she could just blurt all this out. She hadn't thought she would be able to say it out loud. After the initial round of drugs had worn off two days ago, she had mostly just laid there listening to a parade of different people coming in to talk to her, each one smiling, each one more depressing than the last.

"Anyway," Katie said, "I was wondering; how is the high school up in your town?"

"Crap," Alice said, smiling. "It's tribal, and lots of drugs, but the university is good. I spend a lot of time in the university library."

"Hey, Alice?"

"Yep."

"How did you do all that? And why are some people in India interested in you?"

Alice looked at Katie, and then down at the cold tile floor.

"*Siddhis.*"

"Bless you."

"No, my friend said I had yoga *siddhis.*"

"Yoga? Like down-dog, yoga pants and all that?"

"No. It's like…the air is like water for me," Alice said. "It's living and breathing…. It's…a long story."

"With a happy ending?" Katie asked.

"You don't even know me," Alice said, looking up. "I'm supposedly a freak."

"So am I. Just look at me."

"Hey, look in the mirror. You are pretty. They did a good job on you six months ago. I think you look better than you did before."

Katie hadn't dreamed anyone would even think she looked human, let alone pretty.

"And you're a really nice person," Alice added. "You're not a brat anymore."

"Yeah," Katie said, smiling.

"I'll come visit when I pick up my car," Alice said, turning abruptly and walking away. "See ya next week, Katie," she said from the hallway.

"Take care, Alice," Katie said to the empty doorway.

She didn't feel completely alone anymore.

GET TYLER PIKE'S STARTER LIBRARY FOR FREE

If you haven't done so already, sign up now for Tyler's no-spam reading group and get e-book versions of this novella and part one of the full length novel, *Girl in the Air* which is book one of the Alice Brickstone series. You'll also receive many future releases and updates, **all for free**.

Details at www.tylerpikebooks.com